Surprise Moon

by Caroline Hatton
illustrated by Felicia Hoshino

Bebop Books

An imprint of LEE & LOW BOOKS Inc.

D1299505

"It's party time!" said Nick.
"Is it your birthday?" asked Pam.
"No," said Nick. "It's the Autumn Moon Festival."
"What's that?" asked Bob.
"It's a holiday in Vietnam, where my dad is from,"
said Nick.

3

"We can carry lanterns in a parade," said Nick.
"I want the red car," said Pam.
"I want the blue fish," said Nick.
"I don't want the pink butterfly," said Bob.

"You can make noise," said Nick.
"Bang a pan with a big spoon."

Off they went, down the street. *Bang! Bang! Bang!*
The neighbors came out of their houses.
They clapped and watched the parade.
"Cool," said Bob.
"Cool," said Pam.
"Yes," said Nick. "But this is not the best part."

They walked to the park.
The full moon in the sky was very bright.
It was brighter than all the lanterns.
"Cool," said Bob.
"Cool," said Pam.
"Yes," said Nick. "But this is not the best part."

Nick's mom opened her bag.
"Moon cakes," said Nick.
Nick took a bite.
"*This* is the best part!" he said.

Pam and Bob took bites of their moon cakes.
"Yum! It's sweet," said Pam.
"What's the round, yellow thing inside?" asked Bob.
"Egg yolk," said Nick. "It's the moon inside your cake!"
"Cool!" said Pam and Bob.

About the Autumn Moon Festival

The Autumn Moon Festival, or Children's Festival, *Têt-Trung-Thu* (TET-troong-thoo) is one of the most important Vietnamese holidays. In Vietnam, people use a calendar based on the moon's cycle. The Autumn Moon Festival is on the day of the full moon in the eighth month. It often falls in September. To celebrate children carry lanterns and noisemakers in parades, and watch adults do special dances, such as the dragon dance. Treats include moon cakes, candied fruits, and sweetened lotus seeds.